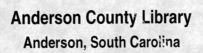

Hop
Jump

Ellen Stoll Walsh

Voyager Books

Harcourt Brace & Company

San Diego   New York   London

First Voyager Books edition 1996
Voyager Books is a registered trademark of
Harcourt Brace & Company.

Library of Congress Cataloging-in-Publication Data
Walsh, Ellen Stoll.
Hop jump/by Ellen Stoll Walsh.—1st ed.
p.   cm.
"Voyager Books."
Summary: Bored with hopping and jumping,
a frog discovers dancing.
ISBN 0-15-292871-5
ISBN 0-15-201375-X pb
[1. Frogs— Fiction. 2. Dancing—Fiction.] I. Title.
PZ7.W1675Ho   1993
[E]—dc20   92-21037

H G

Printed in Singapore

The illustrations in this book are cut-paper collage.
The text type was set in Sabon by Harcourt Brace & Company
Photocomposition Center, San Diego, California.
Color separations by Bright Arts, Ltd., Singapore
Printed and bound by Tien Wah Press, Singapore
This book was printed on Arctic matte paper.
Production supervision by Warren Wallerstein and Ginger Boyer
Designed by Camilla Filancia

For Ben again

"Here they come," said Betsy.

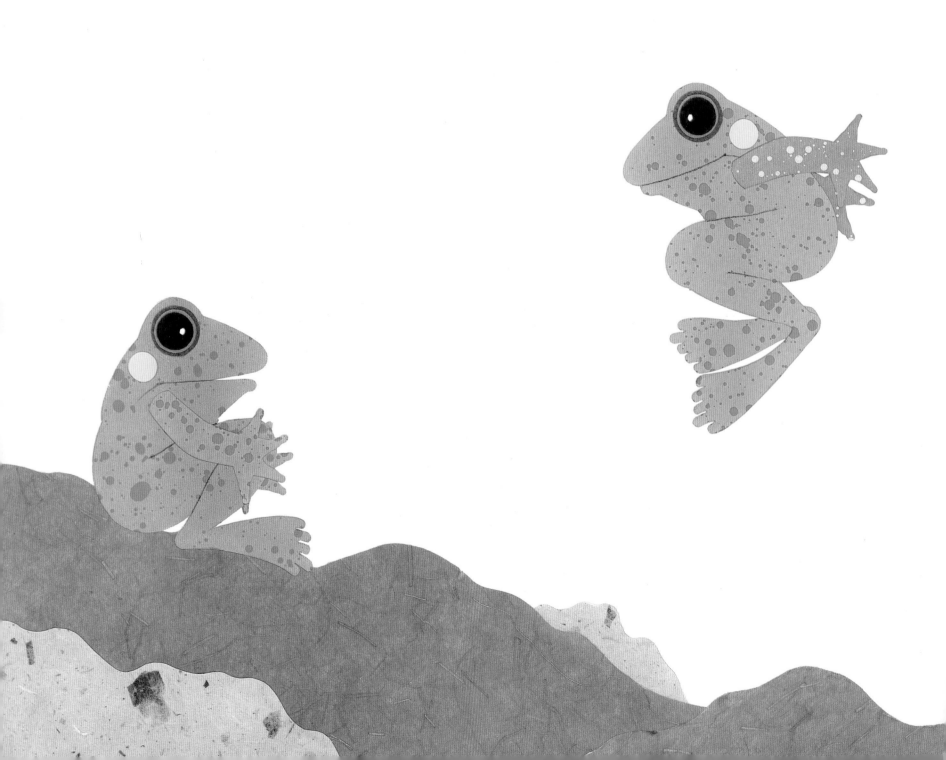

"And there they go. Hop jump, hop jump.
It's always the same," she said.

Betsy watched some leaves float down–
leaping, turning, twisting–always different.

Then Betsy tried. She couldn't float.

But soon she was leaping . . .

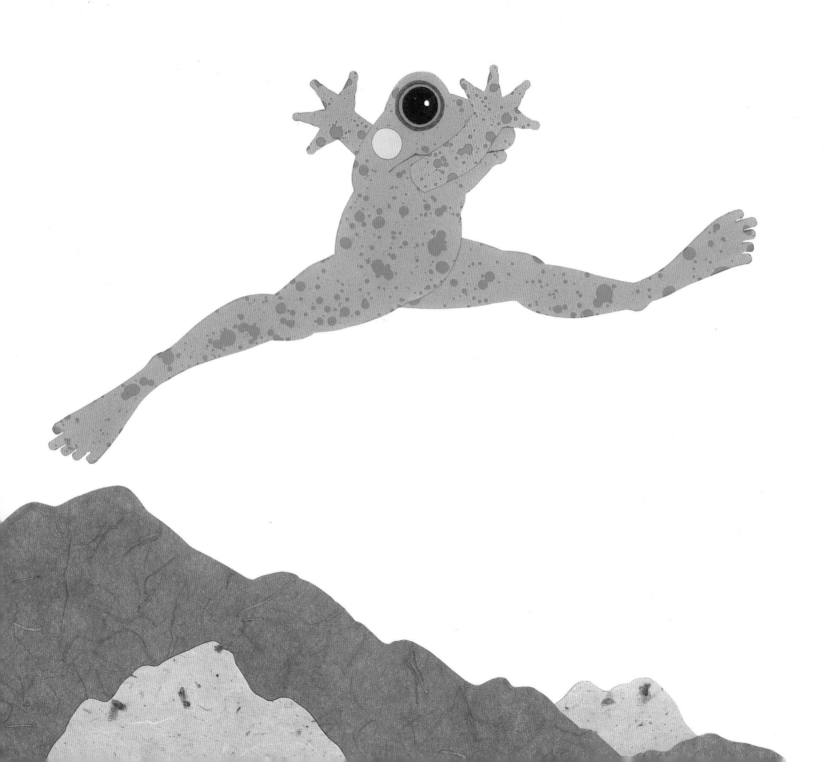

and turning . . .

and twisting.

"It's called dancing," she said.

But along came the other frogs, hop jump, hop jump.

And hop jump, hop jump, back they came again.

"Hey," said Betsy.
"No room for dancing," said the frogs.

"Then I'll find my own place," said Betsy.
"For dancing only."

Some frogs got curious.

Others went to see.

Before long their feet began to move.

Soon all the frogs were dancing.

All but one.
"Hey, no room for hopping," said the frogs.

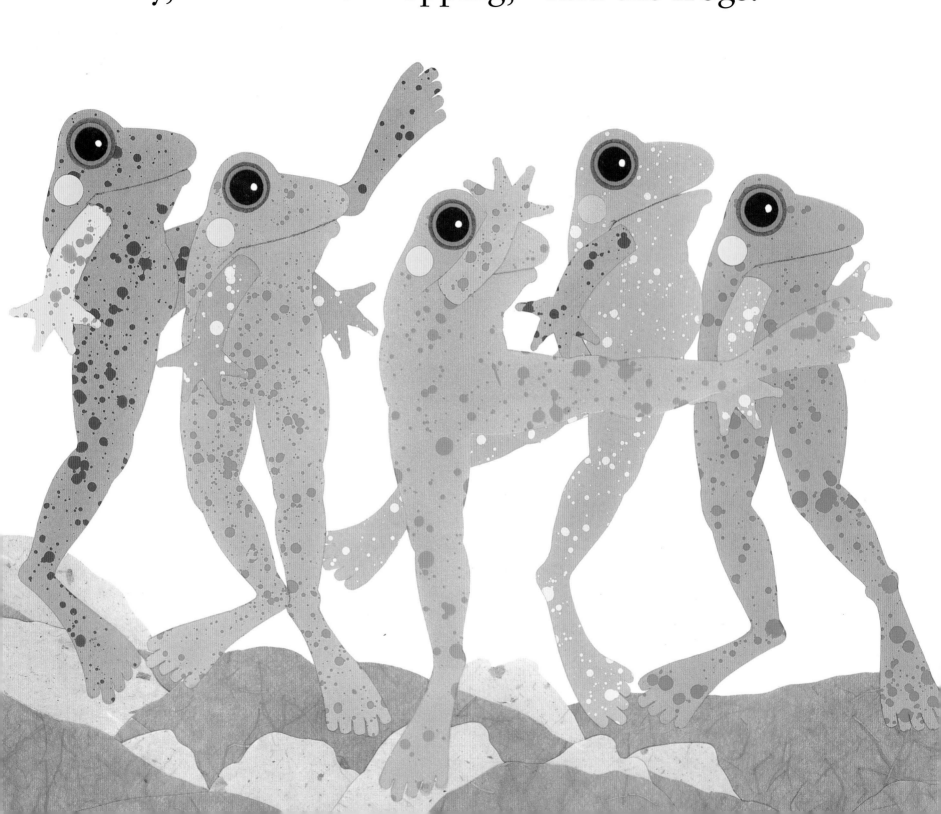

"Oh yes, there's room," said Betsy.
"For dancing and for hopping."

58